Karma Wilson

Illustrated by **Diane Goode**

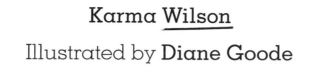

Margaret K. McElderry Books
New York London Toronto Sydney New Delhi

To Shel S.,
who encouraged every child to play with words,
and in doing so, encouraged them to learn how to love,
fight, and reach others with words as well
—K. W.

For Peter
—D. G.

MARGARET K. McELDERRY BOOKS
An imprint of Simon & Schuster Children's Publishing Division
1230 Avenue of the Americas, New York, New York 10020 • This book is a work of fiction. Any references to historical events, real people, or real places are used fictitiously. Other names, characters, places, and events are products of the author's imagination, and any resemblance to actual events or places or persons, living or dead, is entirely coincidental. • Text copyright © 2014 by Karma Wilson • Illustrations copyright © 2014 by Diane Goode • All rights reserved, including the right of reproduction in whole or in part in any form. • MARGARET K. McELDERRY BOOKS is a trademark of Simon & Schuster, Inc. • For information about special discounts for bulk purchases, please contact Simon & Schuster Special Sales at 1-866-506-1949 or business@simonandschuster.com. • The Simon & Schuster Speakers Bureau can bring authors to your live event. For more information or to book an event, contact the Simon & Schuster Speakers Bureau at 1-866-248-3049 or visit our website at www.simonspeakers.com. • Book design by Lauren Rille • The text for this book is set in Memphis. • The illustrations for this book are rendered in brush and pen and ink. Manufactured in the United States of America
0214 FFG
10 9 8 7 6 5 4 3 2 1
Library of Congress Cataloging-in-Publication Data
Wilson, Karma.
Outside the box / Karma Wilson ; illustrated by Diane Goode.
p. cm.
ISBN 978-1-4169-8005-6 (hardcover)
ISBN 978-1-4814-0534-8 (eBook)
I. Title.
PS3623.I5854O98 2013
811'.6—dc23
2011049239

FIRST
EDITION

Welcome!

Welcome to my humble book.
Turn a page and take a look.
I hope you choose to stay awhile,
read a poem, relax, and smile.

But if you find this book a bore,
can't stand to read it anymore,
and tell the world my book is lame,
do me a favor? Forget my name.

Outside the Box

I found a box so neat and square.

It looked so nice inside of there,

sides so straight, dark as night.

"Yes," I said, "it seems just right.

This shall be my thinking spot."

I crawled into the box and thought . . .

and thought . . . .

and thought . . . .

But nothing much popped in my head.

Inside that box, my thoughts were dead.

I heard no sounds, and saw no sights.

I felt alone and missed the light.

There was no color, no cool breeze.

I had to crouch and hug my knees.

I longed for sun and sky and rocks.

I like   to think   outside
the box.

The Great, Big, Fat, Disgusting Lie

It started out so very small,
really, not a lie at all. . . .
No, not a lie . . . more like a fib.
Shall we say a "truth ad lib"?

But as I told the lie, it grew.
And each time someone thought it true,
it changed a little, just a tad.
I'd think of one more thing to add.

Until it finally slipped my head,
the tiny lie I first had said.
And now the lie has grown and grown
and taken on a life of its own.

The lie has grown and I have fed it.
How I wish I'd never said it. . . .

Sick Day

I'm sick, I'm sick!
The doctor said!
Tomorrow there's no school for me!
No projects to do,
no school lunch to chew,
no classes where I have to be.
I'm sick, I'm sick.
The doctor said.
So home is where I get to stay!
Wait, it's Friday? Just my luck.
I'll be sick all Saturday.

A Tragic Poem

Teacher said to write a poem
about a tragedy.
But not a single line or verse
or word would come to me.
I thought and thought and
thought some more,
but thinking did no good.
Teacher said to write a poem
and man, I wish I could!
In the end I wrote a poem
as tragic as can be,
of how I couldn't write a poem
about a tragedy.

My Lucky Number

If I found my lucky number—
just imagine if I did!—
I'd win most every lottery,
I'd be the richest kid!
I'd buy myself a mansion
and my mom a diamond ring.
I'd buy my dad a ton of stuff.
(My sister? Not a thing.)

The Meaning of Lucky

I saw a little clover,
just as pretty as can be.
And when I counted up the leaves,
I counted four, not three!

"I found my lucky clover!
It must be my lucky day!"
I clutched the clover in my hand
and rode my bike away.

I pedaled down the street real fast,
but when I turned the bend,
I didn't see the truck at all!
(I thought it was the end!)

CRASH! BOOM! BASH! My bike was wrecked.
But me? I was okay!
I knew at once without a doubt
my clover saved the day.

And so I told my father
how my clover gave me luck
and saved me almost getting creamed
by an ice cream truck!

My father listened closely
to the tale of my close call.
"If your clover's lucky, son,
then why'd you wreck at all?"

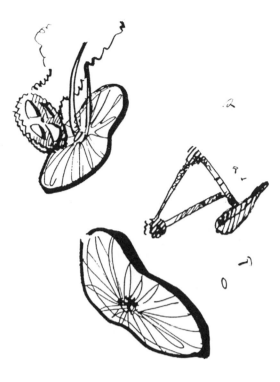

14

Close Shave . . .

I need a razor, I have to shave.
I have some whiskers on my chin.
I saw them in the mirror this morning.
Guess my beard is coming in.
But I won't boast or brag it up.
After all, I just turned ten.

I'm kind of young to have a beard,
but not too young to join the men.
What do you mean it's not a beard?
Why, yes, it is! Look on my chin!
You say that isn't whiskers there?
It's just an old grape jelly smear.
I swear, I swear it looked like hair!

Citizen of the Month

I'm citizen of the month.
I get an award today.
My mom will be so proud!
"That's my son!" she'll say.

I'm citizen of the month.
That's how smart I've been.
I only have one question.
What's a citizen?

Mrs. Crawley's Academy

AWARDS THE

CITIZEN of the MONTH

To _____.

Good Samaritan

Francis Ganley
DIRECTOR

APRIL #1st.

My Pet Robot

I built a robot
just for me,
a friend to keep
me company.
I built him out of
clay and blocks
and sticks and stones
and bits of rocks.
I built him big,
I built him strong,
so tough he'd last
my whole life long!

But now he doesn't
do a lot.
He sits and stares,
my pet robot.
I realize now
that Robot's done. . . .
Building him
was all the fun.

Hide-and-Sleep

I hid myself for hide-and-seek
in a place they'd never guess.
I curled up tight, way out of sight,
beneath my mother's favorite dress.
There in the closet, by the shoes,
I never made a single peep.
I waited, waited, waited . . .
ZZZZZZZZZZZZZZZZZZZZZZZZ
and then I fell asleep.

I ♥ Salad!

I can't wait to eat that salad you're makin'
with crunchy croutons, loads of bacon,
creamy ranch, and bits of cheese.
A side of crusty French bread, please.
I love salad, without a doubt.
(But could you leave the veggies out?)

Bubble Trouble

I bought myself two packs of gum.
I chewed and chewed some more.
I blew a bubble round and fat,
and bigger than ever before!

I blew and it grew
and grew
and grew
and grew!
None of my friends could believe it.
The biggest bubble ever blown,
and I was the kid to achieve it!

I kept on blowing, it kept on growing.
When would it ever stop?
It all seemed like such an awesome plan
till my sister made it
POP!

Stuck in My Head . . .

I have a song that's been stuck in my head
right since I first dragged my feet out of bed.
It's floating around in there loud as can be.
The song will not leave, it keeps pestering me!

It rattles and bounces, it bangs and it taps,
it be-bops and boogies, it jumps and it snaps.
That song is so catchy, it drums and it strums.
It's stuck in my head and I can't help but hum.

It's all I can think of, it's all I can hear.
It's the catchiest song, and I caught it, I fear.
A song so contagious I can't help but sing,
"La la la la, bada bada da bing!"

Come sing it with me, come sing along.
This wonderful, marvelous, fabulous song!
How does it go? Well, now this is absurd. . . .
I've gone and forgotten every last word!

Garage Band

We got ourselves a rake to strum,
a big ol' can that we can drum,
a sprinkler for a microphone,
a whole band we can call our own.
We got the beat, we rock and roll.
We hate to brag, but we got soul.
Introducing . . .

our super, stupendous,
astounding, tremendous,
amaze-you, rock-you,
daze-you, shock-you,
one-of-a-kind . . .
blow-your-mind . . .
garage band!

Now all we need is
a few million fans.

Shower Songs

If you ever sing
in the shower,
sing with your head
pointed down.

For it's true,

dontcha know,

it's a bad way to go . . .

to sing in the shower and drown.

Shhh . . .

Don't scream so loud you wake the dead;
we'd rather that they stay in bed.

Boogie Man

The boogie man is coming.
I can hear him in the night.
He has chains he likes to rattle
when my mom turns out the light.

He is howling, he is prowling.
He is making lots of noise.
He is there inside my toybox.
I think he's haunting all my toys!

The boogie man is coming,
but I'll never scream in fright.
'Cause me and Boogie Man are friends.
We boogie every night. . . .

Werewolves

Werewolves! Where wolves?
Lurking-in-their-lair-wolves!
covered-up-in-hair-wolves,
bright-red-eyes-that-glare-wolves,
wish-they-were-not-there-wolves!

Vampires

They're just an old and silly myth;
I'm not scared of them at all.
They aren't here inside my house.
They aren't lurking down my hall.
They don't have enormous fangs.
They don't roam eternally.
They don't wander thirsting blood.
They don't prowl and search for *me*.
They don't sleep throughout the day,
then come out to hunt at night.
But if vampires do exist,
they're scared of garlic, right?

Sheet!

When you're lying in bed and it's late at night
and there's thumpity-bumps, but no night-light . . .

When your toes are hanging over the bed
and you tremble and shiver and quake with dread . . .

When you're sure you will make a midnight snack
for the monster that's shrouded in shadows so black . . .

Remember:
Just use the force field to cover your feet—
the impenetrable, magical sheet!

39

Alien Under My Bed

There's an alien under my bed.
It's hairy and scary and green.
It's ugly, for sure, all covered with fur.
I bet you it's vicious and mean.

I know that it's not very big.
But it's dangerous all the same.
There's more on the way. They're coming to stay
and insert their probes in our brains!

There's an alien under my bed.
So I pointed it out to my dad.
He just shook his head, laughed, and then said,
"That's just an old sandwich gone bad!"

My friends are all outside. I'd like to tell an inside joke. I've tried

Inside

Joke

and tried and tried. But I can't tell an inside joke. . . .

Professional Liar

I'm a professional liar,
which means I tell lies for a living.
You say that's absurd?
Please, take my word.
(That is, if my word is worth giving!)

I'm a professional liar.
I tell tales most every day.
But I'll shed some light.
My job is to write.
And in *fiction*, lies are okay.

47

Jonathon Allen Baker the Liar

Oh, what a liar, a terrible liar,
was Jonathon Allen Baker the Third.
If Jonathon said it, you'd better forget it.
You couldn't trust one single word!

He once found a dollar, a soggy old dollar,
a wet, dripping dollar he plucked off the street.
But Jonathon said he'd found a gold nugget
that weighed twenty pounds and measured three feet!

He once caught a fish, the tiniest fish,
a fish so darned small it looked like a sardine.
But Jonathon said his fish was a shark,
so big it was almost obscene.

And so he kept lying and telling his stories.
He told us his cuts were wounds from a war.
He told us his grandfather turned tin to gold.
He told us he'd traveled to Saturn before!

So when that boy said he'd be in a movie,
we all rolled our eyes and we laughed like we'd die.
But now I am sitting right here in this theater,
and there on the screen so enormously sized

is Jonathon Allen Baker the Third!
Who would have guessed that his lying would pay?
But as Jonathon says, "I'm not really a liar,
I'm just good at telling the story *my way*."

49

The Tattler

"Teacher, Dale did something bad.
And, Teacher, well, it made us mad.
He shouldn't do that thing he did.
He's really such a rotten kid.
We wish that you would punish Dale
for being such a tattletale!"

My Friend . . . Imaginary

My best imaginary friend
said the rottenest thing to me.
So now I have a super-mean
make-believe enemy!

Thieves

Out somewhere in the dark of night,
where werewolves roam and vampires bite,
past the graveyard, beyond the woods,
draped in capes with shadowy hoods,
they wait. . . .

So go ahead and trick-or-treat
up and down the long, dark streets.
Beg for candy door to door,
but remember, child, what I said before:
They wait. . . .

Sort your candy in a heap,
then go to bed and drift to sleep.
And while you slumber in your bed,
while visions of candy dance in your head,
they come . . .

into the house, and down the hall,
sneaking so well you don't hear them at all.
You'll never, ever know who they are,
but they'll steal the best of your candy bars!

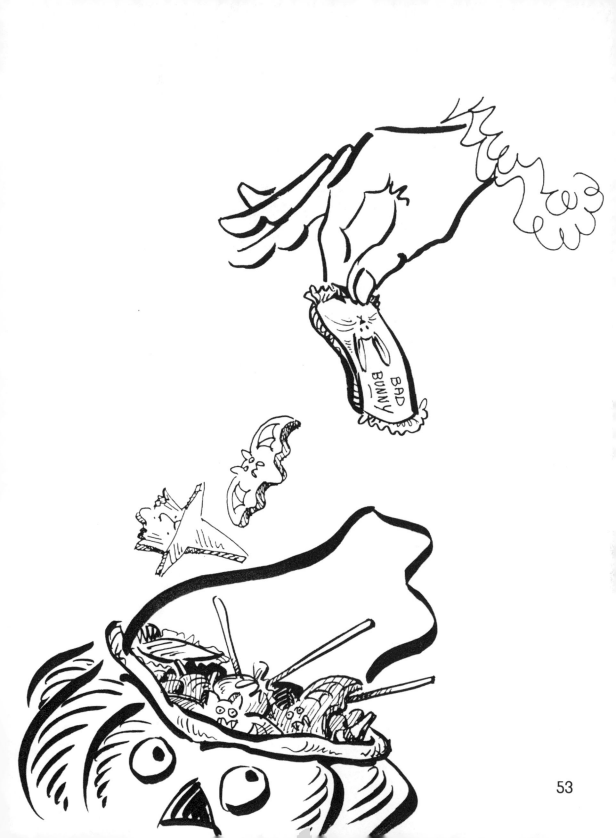

Man in the Moon

When you look at the face
of the Man in the Moon,
what kind of face do you see?
Is it aged and wise, sad, surprised,
or happy and beaming with glee?
Is it angry and stern, full of concern,
wistful, or filled with delight?
What mood do you see
in the face that shines down
and kisses the darkness with light?

The Dream Weaver

Have you heard of the Dream Weaver,
   weaving our dreams
from wishes and rainbows and silver moonbeams?
She lives on a star and she spins from her loom
daydreams from wishes, nightmares from gloom.

Embroidering visions, enriching our nights,
dreams full of magical, mythical sights.
Frightful, wistful, charming, and bleak . . .
each dream, like snowflakes, unique.

The Dream Weaver holds every dream in her hand
and blows them away so they drift down to land.
And where do they fall, where do they go?
There's no need to say. You know. . . .

The Gymnast

He flies through the air
with the greatest of ease.
He flies and he doesn't
need a trapeze!
He dips and darts
through the darkest of night.
He doesn't need nets,
and he doesn't need lights.
He hangs upside down
for hours, no less.
Who is this gymnast?
Who—can you guess?
He sees us in sonar,
imagine that!
The amazing, stupendous
acro . . .
. . . Bat!

59

Ick . . . Gross . . . Ew . . .

All my friends are jealous.
Oh, how they envy me.
I lived through something terrible,
an all-out tragedy!

It happened on the playground.
I was playing all alone,
and then it came and cornered me
and chilled me to the bone!

I tried to run away and hide
but found no way to flee.
I backed into the playground fence
with it pursuing me.

And then the worst thing happened,
an act so dark and bleak.
Mary Ellen Burkenshire
kissed me on the cheek!

EEEEEK!

Somehow I survived it,
and my friends are having fits.
(But I won't tell a single soul,
I liked it . . . just a bit.)

The Fad

He had to have the kind of shoes
that everybody wanted.
The coolest pair a kid could wear,
the kind the rich kids flaunted.
So every day he did odd jobs
before and after school.
He knew that if he owned those shoes
that they would make him cool.
When he'd finally saved enough,
he bought the shoes at last.
He put them on and laced them up
and tried to run real fast.
The shoes weren't very comfortable,
they didn't really fit.
But if they made him popular,
well, he could live with it.
But as he strutted down the halls,
he noticed after a while . . .
nobody else was wearing a pair.
The shoes had gone out of style.

Dorks and Geeks

Dorks and geeks,
artistic freaks,
and nerds *especially*
become the great,
inventive souls
that make our history.

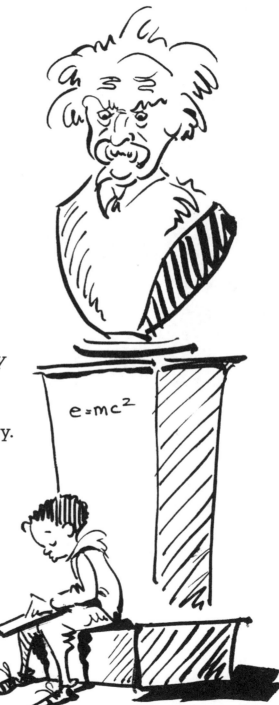

$e = mc^2$

splishing-splashing

plipping-plopping

pitter-patter

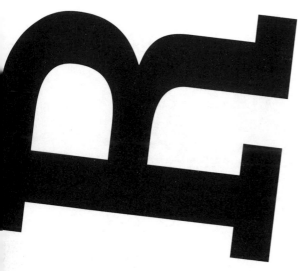

dribble-dropping

Tipping-tapping

rain

singing softly to me

drumming on my windowpane

on the ground

putting puddles

falling down

Leaves

Raking them? No fun at all.
But what a perfect place to fall!

69

A Lump of Clay

It's just a lump of clay,
that's it.
But pick it up
and squeeze a bit.
Now roll it, pat it,
poke it, too.
Pinch the clay
a time or two.
With imagination
and elbow grease,
you'll create
a masterpiece.
Pound it down
to a lump, and then
pick it up and
start again.

71

Oatmeal

As mooshy, gooshy, squishy goo?
It's awful stuff to eat.
As crunchy, munchy cookie bliss?
Oatmeal's a wonderful treat.

Shades of Gray

The shadows of trees, the clouds in the sky.
The wings of a wren as she flutters on by.
The face of the moon as he watches the night,
not quite black, but not quite white.
The hue of the world
when the sun slips away.
Beautiful shades of gray.

Sunrise

Yellow streams, golden beams,
dripping honey-colored light,
shooing away the dark of night.

Globe on fire, rising higher,
beaming, gleaming rays so bright,
shooing away the dark of night.

Morning's begun. Here's the sun!
With dazzling glow the day ignites,
shooing away the dark of night.

Sand!

For making castles, really great,
but in my swimming suit I hate . . .
Sand!
By the sea it looks so pretty,
but it makes my sandwich gritty.
Sand!
I like to run on it a lot,
except for when it gets too hot.
Sand!
Really not much doubt about it,
beaches aren't the same without it.
Sand!

Greekwich

Do you say gyro "yee-roh,"
or does gyro rhyme with "Cairo"?
I'm not sure, but one thing I know
is that it's all Greek to me!

Laugh It Up...

I've often laughed until I cried, bent over, doubled in half.

But I'd really
love it if it if just
one time,
I could cry cry until
I laughed......

Please Don't Feed the Bears

The sign says PLEASE DON'T FEED THE BEARS!
But surely, bears must eat?
It couldn't hurt to feed those bears
a teensy, tiny treat.
A smidge of honey on a roll?
A cracker spread with jam?
A piece of toast, just one at most?
A slice of roasted ham?

The sign says PLEASE DON'T FEED THE BEARS!
So I won't feed them much.
A piece of bread with cheesy spread
and turkey, just a touch.
And then I'll give them spicy chips
and cups of sweet iced tea.
And for dessert, what will they eat?
Oh no, the bears choose me!

Monkey Business

You laugh at the monkeys in the zoo,
but the monkeys laugh right back at you.
While you giggle, point, and stare,
to them you're a monkey without much hair.
So there.

When Naming Crocodiles . . .

A crocodile named Amelia? That I cannot stand!
Name her Margaret, name her Flossy, even name her Fran.
But not Amelia, never that. I must insist you not.
Clear the notion from your head, forget the very thought.
Name her Ella, name her Milly, name her Heloise.
But not Amelia, spare me that, I ask you, pretty please.
Call her dearest, call her sweetheart, call her darling one.
But not Amelia, for I feel that it should not be done.
A crocodile named Amelia? Really, that's a shame.
Why, you ask? I don't like crocs. Amelia is *my* name.

You're No Lady!

The ladybug said,
"You're so dreadfully rude.
Stop calling me *lady*.
Please. I'm a dude!"

Sheep in Wolves' Clothing

The wolves are having trouble
finding tasty sheep to eat.
They wish they could, for sheep taste good;
they have the nicest meat.

But wolves are having trouble,
for the sheep cannot be found.
The sheep are rare, but everywhere,
flocks of wolves abound!

Oh, Deer!

Reindeer are okay, I guess.
But *raindeer* make an awful mess.

Spider Trap

Don't kill helpless spiders if you see 'em.
It's absolutely better if you free 'em.
So never, ever kill those spiders dead.
Set them loose (but in your sister's bed)!

Bear Bare Feet

I wish that I had bare feet.
My toes could wiggle free.
But I'm glad I don't have *bear* feet.
They'd look absurd on me!

Moose on the Bus

There's a moose on the bus,
and he caused quite a fuss
when he clambered aboard, big and brown.
We screamed for police
to restore general peace,
but they weren't anywhere to be found.

The moose thought awhile,
then strolled down the aisle
and sat in the seat next to me.
He is kind, more or less,
and I have to confess,
he makes for polite company.

But one thing I've found
while the bus drives around
and I sit with a moose at my side,
he's friendly and all,
but he's really quite tall,
and his antlers are rather too wide.

The Thing About Puppies . . .

When I got my puppy, I wish I knew
that the things puppies most love to do
are chew . . .
   and chew . . .
     and chew . . .
       and chew . . .
         and poo!

Alan Had a Little Frog

Alan had a little frog,
whose skin was cool and green.
And everywhere that Alan went
the frog was often seen.
He hopped to Alan's school one day,
then turned around and ran
when he saw the science class
dissect amphibians.

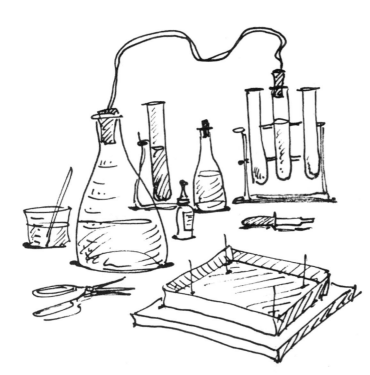

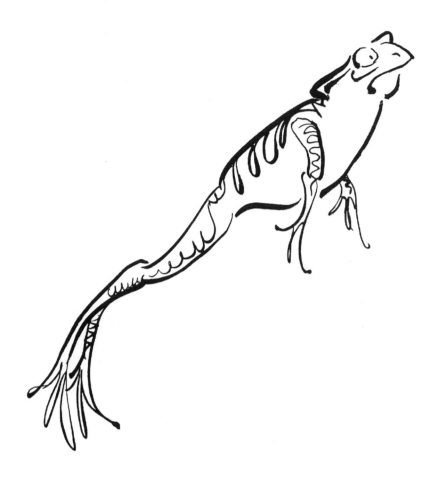

Captain Cluck

Captain Cluck, the pirate duck,
sailed his ship through the seven seas.
He sang as he sailed,
to the fish and the whales,
"It's a pirate's life for me, ho hee!"

Captain Cluck, the pirate duck,
ravaged and pillaged and sacked.
Everyone wondered, but no one dared ask,
why his name wasn't Captain Quack.

Pigasus

Have you ever seen a Pigasus
soar in a midnight sky?
Chances are you never will,
at least until pigs fly.

Stripeless Zebra

Saw a zebra that had no stripes,
a graceful creature, big and white.
My brother only laughed, of course,
and said, "Hey, dork, you saw a horse!"
So I won't bring up the unicorn
I saw today that had no horn.

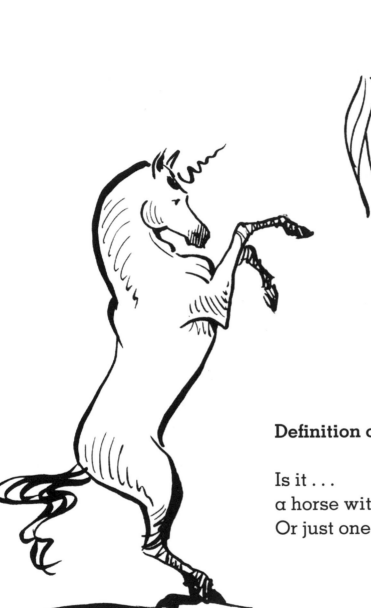

Definition of a Unicorn

Is it . . .
a horse with a horn?
Or just one ear of corn?

107

That Horatio Hipp

Horaceopotamus

Horace Hippopotamus
loved food quite alotamus.
His stomach, it was bottomless.
He ate more than he oughtamus,
that Horace Hippopotamus.

potamus

T. P.

Construction paper, newspaper,
paper boxes, paper bows,
paper plates, paper towels,
paper dolls to cut in rows.

Wrapping paper, wax paper, papier-mâché, pap

es, paper snowflakes oh-so-pretty, taped in windowpanes. Of all these different papers, I do hereby profess ... in my humble opinion, it's true, toilet paper is best.

Master Wrapper

I wrapped a gift picked just for you.
with five rolls of tape and some superglue,
eight kinds of paper, a great shiny bow,
glitter on top, and flowers below!
It looks so lovely, so gorgeous, so pleasant.
Oops! I forgot to put in the present.

Wishy-Washy

The candles flicker brightly
on the tip-top of my cake.
I suck a breath in deeply
and I choose a wish to make.

"I wish Evan liked me!"
(But I say it in my head.)
Then I blow with all my breath
until my face turns red.

The bright flames flicker, flutter,
then softly die away.
My friends all cheer and clap their hands
and shout, "Good job! Hurray!"

But right then Evan picks his nose,
which turns his finger green!
He wipes it on his chair real quick.
He doesn't know I've seen!

I cry, "Relight the candles,
and put them back, all ten!
My first wish was a huge mistake.
I need to trade it in!"

Suckers!

That Edgar J. Mulby, the jerk!
That boy is so totally *ICK*.
He stuck suckers on all of his Valentine cards,
but ones that he'd already licked!

Poor Pete

I have a chocolate bunny
that I'd really love to eat. . . .
But bunny's staring at me,
and he looks so kind and sweet.
Maybe I should keep him.
If I did I'd name him Pete. . . .
CHOMP! Nah . . . I'll just eat him,
and I'm starting with his feet.

Mistaken Identity

One Easter day, I'm sad to say,
a clever kangaroo
stole a key and then, with glee,
he took off from the zoo.
Up and down he hopped through town.
The children yelled and cheered.
Girls and boys declared with joy,
"The Easter Bunny's here!"

Brother's Day

There's Father's Day and Mother's Day,
so I declare a Brother's Day.
A day where brothers everywhere
don't have to do their chores or share.
And homework, well, they breeze right through it:
On that day their sisters do it.
For dinner they just eat dessert. . . .
It's just one day, what can it hurt?
On Brother's Day, obviously,
brothers pick what's on TV.
My brother thinks my idea is grand,
but my sister is not a fan.

A Halloween Secret

Each and every Halloween
the ghosts and ghouls and spooks unseen
don't howl or prowl or roam the night
sniffing for trick-or-treaters to bite. . . .

No! Each and every Halloween
the ghosts and ghouls and spooks unseen
dress up like folks you thought you knew,
teachers, doctors, and principals, too. . . .

They sneak in houses where nobody's home,
and while the trick-or-treaters roam . . .
the ghosts and ghouls and spooks unseen
pass out the candy on Halloween.

124

For Pete's Sake!

Would someone please tell Grandpa Pete
he's much too old to trick-or-treat?

Oh, Tree!

I found the perfect Christmas tree,
growing so majestically,
her branches stretched in silent grace,
bedecked in winter's frosty lace.
She filled the air with spicy scent,
chickadees her ornaments.
I gazed upon that lovely tree,
then turned around and let her be.

The Last Gift

It's the only package left under the tree.
Oh goody, oh goody! A present for me!
My very last gift, I'm sure it's the best.
I know for a fact it will top all the rest.
I shake it and squeeze it. What could it be?
I can't even guess! But soon I will see.
I unwrap so slowly. What is it in there?
Oh, what luck, new underwear. . . .

The Day After

The presents are given,
the stockings are limp.
The candy is eaten
(I feel like a blimp).
The pies are all gone,
the tree is a mess.
I'm sick of the music.
I'm sick of the guests.
I've played with my toys
(I've broken a few).
I've got after-Christmas blues. . . .

ity!

ity,

ing free.

The Law of Gravity

Some laws make no sense to me,

but I love the law of grav

Without the law of grav

we'd all be loose and float

Oh, what a cluttered galaxy,

without the law of gravity.

Flying Low

I'm squished. I'm squashed. I'm bounced. I'm tossed.
I had to turn my cell phone off.
No games to play, not a thing to do.
The movie is boring, and so is the view.
I'm melting in this awful heat.
I didn't get a window seat.
Are we there? Are we done?
Airplane rides are s'posed to be fun!

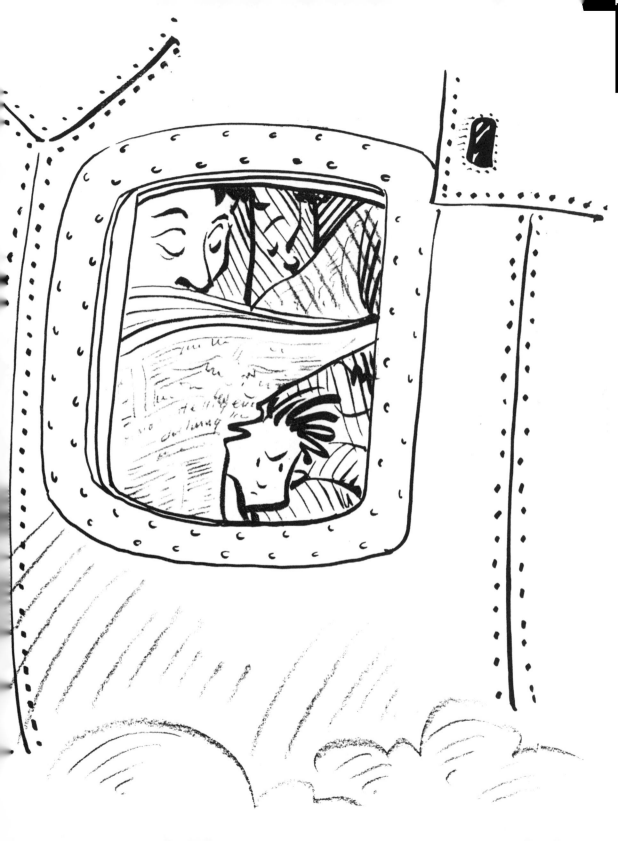

Kite Flying
I flew a kite down by the sea,
until, that is, the kite flew me!
It tugged me high into the sky.
I held on tight and learned to fly!
I felt so free, so featherlight,
flying the world, just me and Kite.

Sledding (Downhill)

I love to sled, I love to sled!
All the trees go zipping by.
Down, down, down the hill I fly.
I hit a jump and bounce so high!
I love to sled, I love to sled!

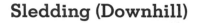

Sledding (Uphill)

I hate to sled, I hate to sled!
Trudging up the hill I go.
Why does uphill go so slow?!
I want to rest and drink cocoa.
I hate to sled, I hate to sled!

The Great Gargantuan

It loops three times, it's blazing fast.
I'm finally tall enough at last!
It's faster than the speed of sound.
It shoots you up, then underground!
I think it goes a mile high,
then it falls straight from the sky.

There's no more line, I'm getting in,
I'll ride the Great Gargantuan.
We climb the hill, so slow . . . so slow.
Then I take a peek below . . .
and *whoooosh*,
straight toward the ground we fly.
This is it, I'm gonna die!

141

We're in a tunnel, black as night.
I'm feeling sick, this isn't right.
Oh no, we're going up once more.
I want my feet back on the floor!
Then down, down, down we fall, fall, fall.
I wish I never rode at all.

142

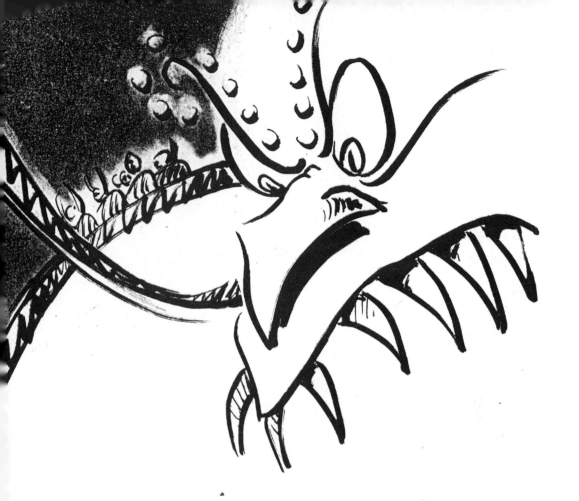

We're slowing down, we're back at last.
Man, that thing goes way too fast.
I rode the Great Gargantuan.
I just can't wait to ride again!

Water-Slide-a-Phobia

I will not ride a water slide.
I do not think I oughta.
Not only am I scared of heights,
I'm terrified of water!

144

Voices in My

Head

I'm hearing **voices** in my head.

They have such **funny** things to say.

The **world** would be a lonely place

if all my voices went away....

Inside, Outside, Upside Down

My brother wore his coat to town
inside, outside, upside down!
Why he put it on that way
I really, truly couldn't say.
He said that's how it fits him best,
with the waist way up there by his chest.
And so he wore his coat to town
inside, outside, upside down.

(My brother makes my mother frown.)

My brother walked down every street
on his hands and not his feet!
I don't think he should walk like that.
It makes it hard to wear a hat.
He said his hands are made to hike
(and you know what my brother's like).

And so he wore his coat to town
inside, outside, upside down,
and walked around on every street
on his hands and not his feet.

(Mother says it's not discreet.)

My brother sat to rest a bit,
but you should see my brother sit.
How he takes a seat, oh dear,
on his head and not his rear!
He said that behinds don't sit best,
and heads are better made to rest.

So he wore his coat to town
inside, outside, upside down.
He walked around on every street
on his hands and not his feet.
He just had to rest a bit
(and we know how my brother sits).

(My mother started having fits!)

At lunch my brother ordered stew
and tried to eat it from his shoe!
He said that bowls are such a bore,
and shoes would spice the flavor more.
His shoes are rather clean and neat,
since he walks on hands, not feet.
And so he wore his coat to town
inside, outside, upside down.
He walked around on every street
on his hands and not his feet.
And he just had to rest a bit.
(Remember how my brother sits?)
Then my brother ordered stew
and tried to eat it from his shoe.

(My mother cried, "What shall I *do*?")

My brother said, "I'll have dessert.
A little bit could never hurt."
But did he order something sweet?
No! He ate a bowl of meat.
"I love a treat of meat to chew.
It tastes so yummy after stew."
He ate his fill, and ate some more.
Then he walked right out the door
on his hands and not his feet.
He made his way back down the street.
He wore his coat, as he left town,
inside, outside, upside down.
And at the park he sat awhile
in his favorite sitting style,
and drank some water from his shoe,
which helped to rinse away the stew.

Then right there in the midst of town,
my brother acted like a clown.
What could make him act this way?
I'm pretty sure I couldn't say.
I always wear my coat about
downside, upside, wrong side out.

(Somehow this makes Father shout.)

The Singer

My sister likes to sing a lot,
but some, like me, prefer she not.

Gamer

He has the high score,
he brags all the time.
He hogs the controller,
I told him it's mine!
We can't watch TV.
Life isn't the same
since Dad discovered
my video game!

The Problem with Baking Cookies

I punched him. He hit me.
I shoved him. He bit me.
I called him a loser.
He called me a goon.
A battle to see which brother would be
the lucky kid who licked off the spoon.

Balloon-a-Phobia

My mother hates balloons, she can't abide 'em.
So if I get balloons, I always hide 'em.
I hid a *huge* one in my brother's room.
My mother sat down on the bed and *BOOM!*
I wonder why my mother hates balloons?

Baby Sis

She cries,
she poops,
she spits stuff up.
She's messy as can be.
And helping change
her diaper, well,
it's not much fun for me.
She keeps the family
up all night,
this crying, squirming girl,
my brand-new little sister,
The Most Beautiful Girl in the World!

Autonomobile

My brother built a car today.
He said, "Hop in. We'll drive away."
Might take a while gettin' there.
The wheels my brother made are square.

Why I Avoid the Kiddie Pool

I have a little brother,
and I'm not a fool.
I know why it's warmer
in the kiddie pool.

Go to Bed

Oh, the dread.
"It's time for bed!"
That is what my mother said.
I asked, "Can I stay up instead?"
My father said, "Go ahead.
Just do a couple chores instead.
Wash the dishes, clean the shed."
"Never mind! I'm off to bed!"

Index of Poem Titles

Index of First Lines

Karma Wilson is the author of *What's the Weather Inside?*, illustrated by Barry Blitt. She also wrote many picture books, including the international bestseller *Bear Snores On*, *Bear Wants More*, *Bear Stays Up for Christmas*, and *Mortimer's Christmas Manger*, all illustrated by Jane Chapman; *A Frog in the Bog*, illustrated by Joan Rankin; and *Hilda Must Be Dancing* and *Bear Hugs*, illustrated by Suzanne Watts. She lives with her family in Fortine, Montana. Visit Karma at KarmaWilson.com.

Diane Goode is the illustrator of more than fifty beloved and critically acclaimed picture books, including the Caldecott Honor Book *When I Was Young in the Mountains* by Cynthia Rylant. She is also the illustrator of *President Pennybaker* and *My Mom Is Trying to Ruin My Life*, both by Kate Feiffer; and the Louise the Big Cheese books by Elise Primavera. Diane lives in Watchung, New Jersey, with her husband, David, and their two dogs, Jack and Daisy.